Bella's Adventure

A Counting Book
From One to Ten

Written By
Kay Publishing

Bella's Adventure

A Counting Book
From One to Ten

By Kay Publishing

This is Bella the bear

Bella is on her way to her friend's party.

Bella has no idea what gift to bring to the party.

"What should I bring to the party?"

Bella is so sad.
She is walking towards
her friend's party
without a gift,

There is **I** little butterfly
come after her journey.

Bella has an idea.
She is thinking of catching the
2 fishes from a pond
and bring them to her
friend's party.

"Oh...there are fishes in the pond"

"Fishes will die before you reach the party". Little butterfly says.

"No Bella, it is not a great idea"

Bella never gives up.
She continues with her journey
and she hopes she could get
the best gift for her friend's
party.

Bella saw an apple tree. She is thinking of grabbing **3** apples from the tree to her friend's party.

"Oh...there are apples on the tree"

The tree is too tall
She could not get the
apples from the
tree.

"opss...the tree is too tall"

Bella continues with her journey again and she hopes she could get
the best gift for her friend's party.

Bella saw **4** little ants are carrying **5** jelly beans.
She is thinking of getting the **5** colorful jelly beans to her friend's party.

"Oh...there are some jelly beans"

Bella continues with her journey again and she hopes she could get the best gift for her friend's party.

Bella saw **6** eggs in a nest.

She is thinking of getting all the **6** eggs to her friend's party.

"Oh...there are some eggs."

Bella continues with her
journey again and she hopes
she could get
the best gift for her friend's
party.

Bella saw **7** starfishes on a beach.

She is thinking of getting all the **7** starfishes to her friend's party.

"Oh...there are some starfishes"

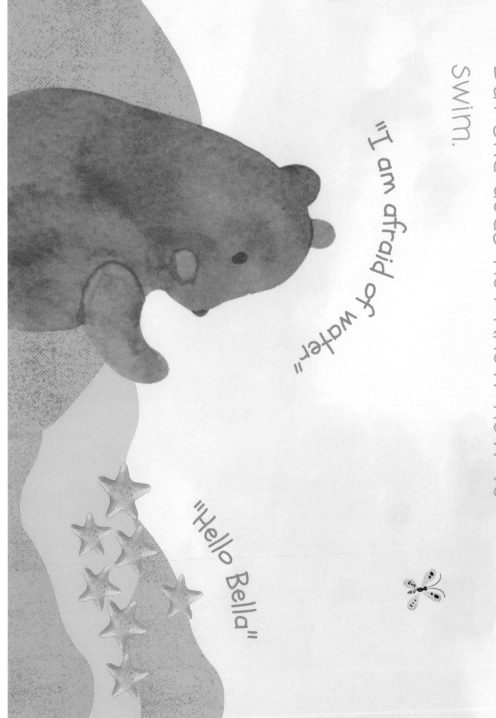

But she does not know how to swim.

"I am afraid of water."

"Hello Bella"

Bella continues with her journey again and she hopes she could get the best gift for her friend's party.

Bella saw **8** carrots on a field.

She is thinking of getting all the **8** carrots to her friend's party.

"Oh...there are some carrots."

Bella continues with her journey again and she hopes she could get the best gift for her friend's party.

Bella saw **9** moths.

She is thinking of catching those moths for her friend's party.

"No Bella, they are my friends."

Bella is very depressed.
She could not get anything for her friend's party.

"Hey Bella, we have something for you"
,the moths say.

"Follow us"

"We can give you **10** planted sunflowers for your friend's party", the moths say.

Bella is so happy with her sunflowers.

She is excited to bring them to the party.

Bella is so contented and she is taking her nap after the party.

Printed in Great Britain
by Amazon